This
Treasure Cove Story
belongs to

PUPPY BIRTHDAY TO YOU!

A CENTUM BOOK 978-1-913865-33-7
Published in Great Britain by Centum Books Ltd.
This edition published 2021.

1 3 5 7 9 10 8 6 4 2

Centum Books Ltd, 20 Devon Square, Newton Abbot,
Devon, TQ12 2HR, UK.

www.centumbooksltd.co.uk | books@centumbooksltd.co.uk
CENTUM BOOKS LIMITED. Reg. No. 07641486.

A CIP catalogue record for this book is available
from the British Library.

Printed in China.

centum

A Treasure Cove Story

PUPPY BIRTHDAY TO YOU!

Based on the screenplay *Pups Turn On the Lights*
by Scott Albert

Illustrated by Fabrizio Petrossi

One windy afternoon in Adventure Bay, a box moved down the street toward Katie's Pet Parlour. But this box wasn't being blown by the wind. *It was creeping down the street on eight paws!*

Suddenly, a big gust blew the box away, revealing Skye and Rubble underneath. They quickly scampered into the shop.

Inside, Ryder, Katie and Rocky were getting ready for Chase's surprise birthday party.

'Who's making sure Chase doesn't surprise *us* while we set up?' Skye asked.

'Marshall,' Rocky said. 'He can keep a secret – can't he?'

Across town, Marshall and Chase were playing in Pup Park. They swung on the swings and slid down the slide.

'Maybe we should go find Ryder and the pups,' Chase said.

'No!' Marshall protested. 'We can't! Because it's, um, so nice out.'

Just then, the wind picked up again and blew them right across the park!

Back at the Pet Parlour, the lights suddenly
went dark, and Katie's mixer stopped.
   'All the lights on the street are out!'
Rocky yelped.
   Ryder thought he knew what was wrong.
'PAW Patrol, to the Lookout!'

The team raced to the Lookout. But without
electricity, the doors wouldn't open. Luckily, Rocky
had a screwdriver, which did the trick.

Once they were inside, Ryder used his telescope to check Adventure Bay's windmills.

'Just as I thought,' he said. 'The wind broke a propeller. Since the windmill can't turn, it can't make electricity. We need to fix it!'

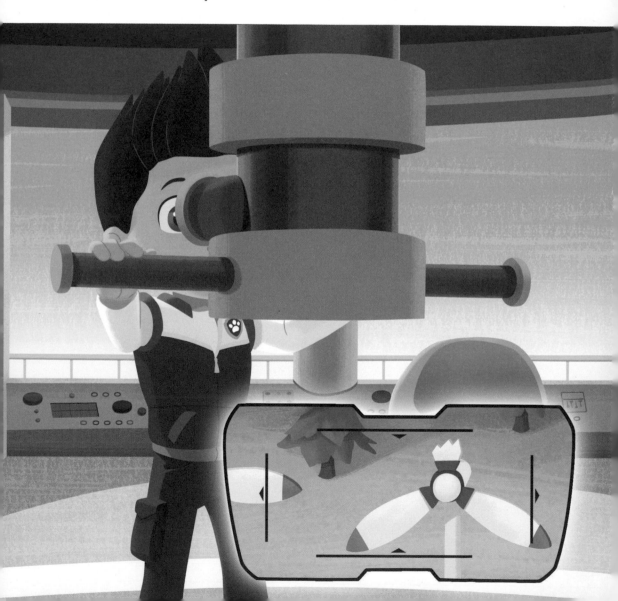

Ryder looked at Rocky. 'We'll need something from your truck to fix the broken blade.'

'Green means go!' Rocky said, preparing for action.

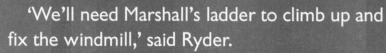

'We'll need Marshall's ladder to climb up and fix the windmill,' said Ryder.

Marshall nodded. 'I'm fired up!'

'Chase, the traffic lights won't work without electricity,' Ryder continued. 'I need you to use your siren and megaphone to direct traffic.'

'These paws uphold the laws,' Chase declared.

Meanwhile, Skye, Zuma and Rubble raced back
to the Pet Parlour to continue setting up for Chase's
surprise party. It was very dark, but Katie had
a torch.

At the centre of town, Chase busily directed traffic.
'You're our hero,' Mayor Goodway said as she crossed
the street safely.
'I'm just doing my PAW Patrol duty,' Chase said.

Up in the hills, Ryder, Marshall and Rocky went
to work on the broken windmill. Ryder climbed
Marshall's ladder and removed the old blade while
Rocky looked for a replacement piece.

'No, not a tyre… not a garden chair,' Rocky said,
pulling stuff out of his truck. At last he found what
he wanted. 'Here it is – my old surfboard!'

'This surfboard will catch a breeze and help turn it into electricity,' Rocky said as he bolted the board into place. The wind picked up and the windmill started to turn. Lights came on all over Adventure Bay!

The traffic lights started working again. 'Ryder and the PAW Patrol did it!' Chase announced through his megaphone. 'My work here is done!'

The lights in the Pet Parlour glowed brightly.
'Hooray!' cheered Skye, but then she frowned.
'Aw! There's no time to make a cake.'
Katie thought for a moment. 'I have an idea!'

As Chase drove back to the
Lookout, he got a call from Ryder.
'We need you at Katie's – in a hurry!'

When Chase got
there, everything
was dark and quiet.

Chase stepped inside. The lights went on.
'SURPRISE!' everyone yelled.
Chase was amazed. 'Wow! You guys turned
the lights back on AND made a party for me?'
'We didn't have time to bake you a real cake,' Katie
said, 'so we hope you like your pup-treat cookie cake.'

'Whenever it's your birthday, just yelp
for help!' Ryder said with a laugh.
All the puppies cheered and enjoyed
a taste of Chase's special cake.

Treasure Cove Stories

Please contact Centum Books
to receive the full list of titles in
the *Treasure Cove Stories* series.
books@centumbooksltd.co.uk

1 Three Little Pigs
2 Snow White and
the Seven Dwarfs
3 The Fox and the Hound
- Hide-and-Seek
4 Dumbo
5 Cinderella
6 Cinderella's Friends
7 Alice in Wonderland
8 Mad Hatter's Tea Party
from Alice in Wonderland
9 Mickey Mouse and
his Spaceship
10 Peter Pan
11 Pinocchio
12 Mickey and the Beanstalk
13 Sleeping Beauty
and the Good Fairies
14 The Lucky Puppy
15 Chicken Little
16 The Incredibles
17 Coco
18 Winnie the Pooh and Tigger
19 The Sword in the Stone
20 Mary Poppins
21 The Jungle Book
22 Aristocats
23 Lady and the Tramp
24 Bambi
25 Bambi - Friends of the Forest
26 Pete's Dragon
27 Beauty and the Beast
- The Teapot's Tale
28 Monsters, Inc.
- M is for Monster
29 Finding Nemo
30 The Incredibles 2
31 The Incredibles
– Jack-Jack Attack
32 Ratatouille – Your Friend the Rat
33 Wall-E
34 Up
35 The Princess and the Frog

36 Toy Story – The Pet Problem
39 Spider-Man – Night of the Vulture!
40 Wreck it Ralph
41 Brave
42 The Invincible Iron Man
– Eye of the Dragon
45 Toy Story – A Roaring Adventure
46 Cars – Deputy Mater Saves the Day!
49 Spider-Man – High Voltage!
50 Frozen
51 Cinderella is my Babysitter
52 Beauty and the Beast
- I am the Beast
56 I am a Princess
57 The Big Book of Paw Patrol
58 Paw Patrol
- Adventures with Grandpa!
59 Paw Patrol - Pirate Pups!
60 Trolls
61 Trolls Holiday
63 Zootropolis
64 Ariel is my Babysitter
65 Tiana is my Babysitter
66 Belle is my Babysitter
67 Paw Patrol
- Itty-Bitty Kitty Rescue
68 Moana
70 Guardians of the Galaxy
71 Captain America
- High-Stakes Heist!
72 Ant-Man
73 The Mighty Avengers
74 The Mighty Avengers
- Lights Out!
75 The Incredible Hulk
78 Paw Patrol - All-Star Pups!
80 I am Ariel
82 Jasmine is my Babysitter
87 Beauty and the Beast - I am Belle
88 The Lion Guard
- The Imaginary Okapi
89 Thor - Thunder Strike!
90 Guardians of the Galaxy
- Rocket to the Rescue!
93 Olaf's Frozen Adventure
94 Black Panther
95 Trolls - Branch's Bunker Birthday
96 Trolls - Poppy's Party

97 The Ugly Duckling
98 Cars - Look Out for Mater!
99 101 Dalmatians
100 The Sorcerer's Apprentice
101 Tangled
105 The Mighty Thor
106 Doctor Strange
107 Captain Marvel
108 The Invincible Iron Man
109 Black Panther
- Warriors of Wakanda
110 The Big Freeze
111 Ratatouille
112 Aladdin
113 Aladdin - I am the Genie
114 Seven Dwarfs Find a House
115 Toy Story
116 Toy Story 4
117 Paw Patrol - Jurassic Bark!
118 Paw Patrol
- Mighty Pup Power!
121 The Lion King - I am Simba
122 Winnie the Pooh
- The Honey Tree
123 Frozen II
124 Baby Shark and the
Colours of the Ocean
125 Baby Shark and
the Police Sharks!
126 Trolls World Tour
127 I am Elsa
128 I am Anna
129 I am Olaf
130 I am Mulan
131 Sleeping Beauty
132 Onward
133 Paw Patrol
– Puppy Birthday to You!
134 Black Widow
135 Trolls - Poppy's Big Day!
136 Baby Shark and the Tooth Fairy
137 Baby Shark – Mummy Shark
138 Inside Out
139 The Prince and the Pauper
140 Finding Dory
141 Cars - Travel Buddies
142 The Lion King
- Simba's Daring Rescue

Book list may be subject to change. Not all titles are listed.